PRESENTS

THE AMERICAN GIRLS COLLECTION ®

17 74

MEET FELICITY · An American Girl
FELICITY LEARNS A LESSON · A School Story
FELICITY'S SURPRISE · A Christmas Story

18 54

MEET KIRSTEN · An American Girl
KIRSTEN LEARNS A LESSON · A School Story
KIRSTEN'S SURPRISE · A Christmas Story
HAPPY BIRTHDAY, KIRSTEN! · A Springtime Story
KIRSTEN SAVES THE DAY · A Summer Story
CHANGES FOR KIRSTEN · A Winter Story

19 04

MEET SAMANTHA · An American Girl
SAMANTHA LEARNS A LESSON · A School Story
SAMANTHA'S SURPRISE · A Christmas Story
HAPPY BIRTHDAY, SAMANTHA! · A Springtime Story
SAMANTHA SAVES THE DAY · A Summer Story
CHANGES FOR SAMANTHA · A Winter Story

19 44

MEET MOLLY · An American Girl
MOLLY LEARNS A LESSON · A School Story
MOLLY'S SURPRISE · A Christmas Story
HAPPY BIRTHDAY, MOLLY! · A Springtime Story
MOLLY SAVES THE DAY · A Summer Story
CHANGES FOR MOLLY · A Winter Story

FELICITY
LEARNS
A LESSON

A School Story

BY VALERIE TRIPP

ILLUSTRATIONS DAN ANDREASEN

VIGNETTES LUANN ROBERTS, KEITH SKEEN

PLEASANT COMPANY

PICTURE CREDITS
The following individuals and organizations have generously given
permission to reprint illustrations contained in "Looking Back":
pp. 64-65—Colonial Williamsburg Foundation; Smithsonian Institution Photo No. 76-
9331; Independence National Historical Park Collection, Philadelphia; Colonial
Williamsburg Foundation; pp. 66-67—Philip and Charlotte Hanes; Colonial
Williamsburg Foundation (sampler); pp. 68-69—North Wind Picture Archives; Colonial
Williamsburg Foundation; The Granger Collection, New York; Colonial Williamsburg
Foundation; American Philosophical Society, Philadelphia.

Edited by Jeanne Thieme
Designed by Myland McRevey and Michael John Victor
Art Directed by Kathleen A. Brown

Library of Congress Cataloging-in-Publication Data

Tripp, Valerie, 1951-
Felicity learns a lesson : a school story / by Valerie Tripp ; illustrations, Dan Andreasen ;
vignettes, Luann Roberts, Keith Skeen.

p. cm. — (The American girls collection)
Summary: Shortly before the Revolutionary War, nine-year-old Felicity, who lives in
Williamsburg, is torn between supporting the tariff-induced tea boycott and saving her
friendship with Elizabeth, a young loyalist from England.

ISBN 1-56247-006-X — ISBN 1-56247-007-8 (pbk.)
[1. Virginia—Social life and customs—Colonial period, ca. 1600-1775—Fiction.
2. Friendship—Fiction.]
I. Andreasen, Dan, ill.   II. Title.   III. Series.
PZ7.T7363Fe   1991   [Fic]—dc20   91-11659   CIP   AC

TO ELIZABETH AND SASHA

TABLE OF CONTENTS

FELICITY'S FAMILY

FATHER
Felicity's father, who owns one of the general stores in Williamsburg.

MOTHER
Felicity's mother, who takes care of her family with love and pride.

FELICITY
A spunky, spritely colonial girl, growing up just before the American Revolution in 1774.

NAN
Felicity's sweet and sensible sister, who is six years old.

WILLIAM
Felicity's almost-three brother, who likes mischief and mud puddles.

BEN DAVIDSON
*A quiet apprentice
living with the
Merrimans while
learning to work in
Father's store.*

MISS MANDERLY
*Felicity's teacher—
a gracious gentlewoman.*

ELIZABETH COLE
*Felicity's best friend is
new to the colonies and
admires Felicity.*

ANNABELLE COLE
*Elizabeth's snobby older
sister who thinks
everything in England
is better.*

ROSE
*The cook and
maidservant at the
Merrimans'.*

—

APPLE BUTTER DAY

Felicity Merriman sat high atop the roof of her house and tilted her face up to the sun. The rooftop was a fine place to be on a bright blue October morning like this.

Felicity leaned back against the chimney. She put one leg on either side of the steep roof. The shingles were warm against her bare legs. A restless breeze played with her petticoats. Felicity shaded her eyes with her hand and looked out over the treetops and rooftops of Williamsburg. She watched a bright red cardinal bird swoop across the sky. Felicity grinned. *How lovely it must feel to fly wherever you want to go, with nothing holding you down,* she thought.

"Lissie! Lissieeee!" she heard her sister Nan calling her.

Felicity decided to ignore Nan. She knew what Nan wanted. Today was apple butter day. That's why Felicity was on the roof. She was supposed to be picking apples for Mother to make into apple butter. The best apples were at the very top of the tree, where the branches hung over the roof. So Felicity had fetched a ladder, climbed up to the roof, and filled her apple sack quickly and easily. Now Nan wanted *her* turn to pick apples. She wanted Felicity to work in the hot, stuffy kitchen, stirring the pot of sticky apple mush. Felicity was not ready to go in.

Felicity pulled one of the apples out of the sack and rubbed it on her sleeve. She took a big bite. Mmmm! Felicity seemed to taste the warm summer sun, the wild rains of September, and the cool, dark, starry nights of autumn in that juicy, tart bite. Between chews, Felicity wiggled her loose tooth with her thumb. She couldn't wait for it to fall out. Ben, her father's apprentice, was teaching her to whistle with her fingers in her mouth. She thought losing that tooth might help.

Felicity tried whistling. *If I whistled loud enough,* she thought, *Nan and everyone in Williamsburg would hear me. They'd see me up here on the roof, as high as a flag!* She smiled. *Wouldn't that be fine?*

"Lissie!" she heard Nan call again. "Where are you?"

"I'm up here," Felicity answered. She waved to Nan from her perch.

"Lissie!" yelped Nan. She sounded scared. "Mother!" she called. "Come quick! Lissie's on the *roof!* Mother! Come and see."

"Whatever's the matter, Nan?" asked Mrs.

3

Merriman. She rushed out of the kitchen. Felicity's brother, William, toddled along behind her. "*What's on the roof?*" She looked up. When she saw Felicity, she gasped. "Oh my gracious! Lissie!" Then she said in a very stern voice, "Felicity Merriman, I will not shout for all the world to hear. Come down from that roof immediately."

"Yes, Mother," said Felicity. She slid down the roof to the ladder with a sinking feeling. *I've done something wrong-headed again,* she thought to herself. Felicity scrambled down the ladder so quickly she scraped her knee, lost her footing, and had to jump the last few feet to the ground.

When she landed, her mother felt her all over as if she might have broken bones. "Goodness, Lissie!" she said. "You gave me such a fright! Climbing way up on the roof like that! What were you thinking of?"

"Well, I . . . well, it didn't *seem* dangerous," said Felicity. "And there were so many more apples at the top of the tree."

"So you thought you could fetch the apples faster. Is that it? Impatient as usual," said her mother. She put her hands on Lissie's shoulders and said gently but firmly, "You are near to ten years of age, Felicity. That's old enough to know what's a danger to you. And that's too old to be acting careless and childish."

Felicity shifted the heavy apple sack off her shoulder. "I'm sorry . . ."

"I know you are," said her mother kindly. "But I do wish you would stop and think before you act. Sometimes you have no more sense than a giddy goose!" She sighed. "And let us hope no one saw you on the roof with your petticoats blowing above your knees, bare-legged as a newborn babe. 'Tis wrong and unseemly for a girl your age. Now put your shoes and stockings on and come inside quick as you can. Nan will finish picking the apples."

Felicity trailed along behind her mother to the kitchen house. Her heart was as heavy as the apple sack. The kitchen was dark compared to outside. The air was hot and thick. Rose, the cook, was peeling apples, slicing them into four parts, and dropping them in a pot of water. Another big pot full of apple mush was burbling by the fire. Mrs. Merriman pointed to it.

"You stir, Lissie," she said. "Don't let the apples stick to the pot. And mind you don't scorch your petticoat by the fire."

Felicity stirred with a long wooden spoon. Round and round, again and again, she stirred the apple mush till her arms ached. It was tiresome work, and dull. Her hair stuck to her sweaty neck. Her hands were sore, and her back was stiff. As soon as one batch of apples was cooked soft, Rose took it away and put another pot on the fire. Felicity tried to hide her impatience. But after a while, she could not help asking, "Isn't that enough? Haven't we made hundreds of pounds of apple butter by now?"

"Goodness, no," said her mother. "A whole pound of apples makes only one pint of apple butter."

Pints were very small. Felicity sighed. "It seems to be a great deal of work for a little bit of butter. I don't think it's worthwhile," she said. "And once the apple butter's eaten, there's nothing to show for all the hard work. You are left with nothing at all."

Mrs. Merriman laughed. "I remember thinking just that same thing when I was your age," she said. "And 'tis true, there's nothing left that anyone can see. But I know that I've provided for my family, and that pleases me." She looked kindly at Felicity. "Caring for a family is a responsibility and a pleasure. It will be your most important task, and one that you must learn to do well. I want you to be a notable housewife when you are grown."

"Notable?" asked Felicity.

"Yes," said Mrs. Merriman. "A notable housewife runs her household smoothly, so that everyone in it is happy and healthy. Her life is private and quiet. She is content doing things for her family."

"Things nobody ever sees," said Felicity.

"Aye," agreed her mother. "But many lovely things are private and hidden." She picked up one of the apples. "Look," she said. She sliced the apple in half across its fat middle, instead of top to bottom. She held the halves up to Felicity. "Have you ever seen the flower that is hidden inside every apple?" she asked. "It's there for those who know how to find it. See?"

Felicity grinned at her mother. There was indeed a flower inside the apple.

"My mother showed that to me when I was a girl and we made apple butter together," said Mother. "She taught me to sew and cook and plant a garden and run a household. Now I am teaching you. Someday you will teach your daughter."

"Oh, dear," said Felicity. "It seems a great deal to learn!"

"Indeed, yes," said Mrs. Merriman. "And that is not all you must know how to do. When I was just about your age, I had special lessons with my aunt. She taught me the proper way to act in polite society. She showed me how to serve tea and how to be a gracious hostess." She smiled at the memory. "How I loved those lessons with my aunt! I felt like a graceful young lady instead of a gawky little girl."

Felicity wiggled her tooth. She didn't say anything, but the lessons her mother described sounded fussy to her.

Mrs. Merriman looked at Felicity thoughtfully. "Perhaps it is time for you . . ." she began. Then she caught sight of the pot of apple mush. "Mercy!"

she said. "*Stir,* Lissie! This batch is near to burning!" And she did not finish the sentence she had begun.

But a few nights later, Felicity found out what her mother had been about to say. It was after supper. Everyone was gathered in the parlor around the fire. Its warmth was welcome, for the sun set early these fall evenings, and the dusk was chilly. Felicity sat on a low stool next to Nan. She was helping Nan learn to read the Lord's Prayer printed on her hornbook.

Nan tilted the hornbook toward the firelight. "'. . . Thy kingdom come,'" she read slowly. "Lissie," she asked. "Whose kingdom do we live in? God's or the King of England's?"

"Well, both, I suppose," answered Felicity. "Isn't that right, Father?"

Mr. Merriman was holding William on his knee and playing chess with Ben, the young apprentice who helped Mr. Merriman at his store. He looked over at his daughters and nodded. "Aye," he said. "We live in the colony of Virginia, which belongs to the King of England. He rules us, even though he lives far away. Virginia is part of his kingdom."

"But Virginia is part of God's kingdom, too," said Felicity. "Because the whole world, and heaven, and all the stars and everything there is belongs to God. See what it says here, in the rest of the prayer: 'Thy will be done on earth as it is in heaven.' That means God rules both heaven and earth."

"Which word says heaven?" asked Nan.

"This one right here," said Felicity. She pointed to it and read, "Heaven, H - E - A - V - E - N."

"You can read *everything*, can't you, Lissie?" asked Nan.

"Not everything, not yet," said Felicity. "But I do love to read. I'd like to attend the college here in Williamsburg, and read Greek and Latin and philosophy and geography, just as the young gentlemen do."

"Oh, Lissie," laughed Nan. "That's silly! Girls aren't taught at the college."

Ben looked up from the chessboard and grinned. "Maybe you could pretend to be a boy," he said. "I have a pair of breeches you may borrow."

Felicity grinned back, but then she sighed. "I don't see why girls aren't educated, too."

Mrs. Merriman looked up from her stitching and spoke. "Girls *should* be educated. Not in Latin and Greek, but in the things they need to know to be accomplished young ladies." She looked at Mr. Merriman with a question in her eyes.

Mr. Merriman nodded and smiled. Then he said in a very pleased voice, "Felicity, your mother and I have decided it is time for you to begin *your* education."

Felicity sat up. "Am I to be apprenticed, Father?" she asked hopefully. Some girls were apprentices. They learned to be seamstresses, or to make hats, or even to work in shops. Felicity had always dreamed of working in her father's store.

"Goodness, no!" exclaimed her mother. "You are fortunate enough to be the daughter of Edward Merriman, one of Williamsburg's most important merchants. You are to be educated as a *gentlewoman*."

"Oh," said Felicity. She was disappointed. "What am I to learn?"

"Girls should be educated," Mrs. Merriman said,
"so they can grow up to be accomplished gentlewomen."

"The things my aunt taught me," answered Mrs. Merriman. "You will have lessons in dancing, handwriting, fancy stitchery, the proper way to serve tea—"

"Tea?" interrupted Ben. "Lessons about serving tea?"

"Indeed, yes!" said Mrs. Merriman. "A lady's manners are judged by the way she serves tea. My mother brought her best teapot with her when she left England to come to Virginia. She used to say the king himself would feel at home at her tea table. She served tea as properly in Virginia as any lady did in London. Now Felicity must learn to serve tea properly, too."

"Tea and stitchery!" sighed Nan. "The lessons sound lovely!"

"I'm not very good at those quiet, sitting down kinds of things," said Felicity.

"Well," said Mrs. Merriman calmly. "Then you must improve yourself."

Felicity was beginning to feel trapped. She asked, "Who will be my teacher?"

"A very respectable gentlewoman named Miss Manderly," said Mr. Merriman. "She is going to give lessons to two other young ladies. They are sisters, and their family has just come here from England. Miss Manderly has kindly agreed to let you join them."

"Ooooh!" squealed Nan. "Young ladies from England! They'll probably already know the very most proper way to do everything, Lissie!"

"The young ladies from England will be learning from Miss Manderly just as Felicity will," said Mr. Merriman. "And they will surely learn that proper and polite behavior is the same in Virginia as it is in England."

Felicity sighed. She could see that these lessons were going to be boring and tiresome. *I would much rather spend my time out of doors*, she thought. *I would rather be horseback riding, or playing, or digging in my garden.* But Felicity knew she could not argue, or pout, or say she would *not* go to Miss Manderly's. That would not be respectful. Besides, Felicity was sure it would do no good at all.

"The lessons begin in three days' time," said Mrs. Merriman. "So we must set to work tomorrow to make ready your best cap and stockings and clothes."

"Aye!" agreed Mr. Merriman. He smiled at Felicity fondly. "Our pretty Lissie must look her very best. She will begin her lessons looking like the finest young lady in Virginia, and all of England, too. She will make us proud, to be sure."

Felicity smiled back weakly. She was not at all sure. She pushed against her loose tooth with her tongue until it hurt.

LOOSE TOOTH TEA

"Stand still, my child," said Mrs. Merriman for the hundredth time. She and Nan were kneeling on the floor, checking to be sure the hem of Felicity's outer petticoat was even. This was the day Felicity was to begin her lessons.

"Mother," said Felicity impatiently. "How will Miss Manderly know if my hem is even or not? Why does it matter?"

Mrs. Merriman sat back on her heels and looked Felicity in the eye. "Everything has to be perfect. I won't have the two young ladies from England thinking we don't know how to dress ourselves here in the colonies," she said. "I want

them to see that though we may live on the edge of
the wilderness, we are just as civilized as they are."
She sounded very determined.

Felicity sighed. For the past three days she had
been scrubbed and scoured. Her face had been
washed with buttermilk to make the skin soft. Her
nose had been rubbed with lemon juice to bleach
out the freckles. Her hair had been twisted up on
clay rollers and combed through with a pomade of
hog's fat and cinnamon. Her clothes had been let
out and taken in, taken up and let down, washed,
mended, starched, and ironed till they were stiff
with perfection. It was all very tiresome. Felicity
wiggled her tooth. Now she could push it into her
lip. It was going to fall out soon. *Not much longer*,
she thought.

"Not much longer, my dear," said her mother
as she fastened Felicity's coral necklace around her
neck. "I'm almost through with you."

"Oh, Lissie," said Nan. "You look pretty. You
really do."

Mrs. Merriman stepped back and studied
Felicity from head to toe. Then she said, "Nan is
right. Felicity Merriman, you look as pretty as can

be." She looked pleased.

Felicity smiled. One of her garters was tied too tight. The laces on her bodice were tight, too. She felt nervous and uncomfortable and too clean, but it was almost worth it to see her mother so pleased.

"Off you go to Miss Manderly's," said Mrs. Merriman. "It won't do to be late. And I won't have you galloping there to arrive flushed and mussy." She gave Felicity's hat one last touch. "Now remember to stop by the store so Ben can escort you. And remember to sit up straight."

"Remember your handkerchief!" added Nan.

"Go along, now," said Mrs. Merriman, shooing Felicity towards the door. "Don't forget to speak softly. Remember your gloves. And remember . . ." She stopped.

Felicity looked back, waiting for her to finish.

"Remember that you are my dear daughter and I am very proud of you," said Mrs. Merriman. "Now off you go!"

Her mother's praise cheered Felicity as she hurried along the busy street. Williamsburg was crowded now, because it was Public Times. People from all over the colony came to Williamsburg for business and pleasure at Public Times. They came to hear the trials in the law courts and to catch up on all the news. There were balls and parties and markets and plays. The shops were busy. The taverns were full of visitors from out of town. The streets were noisy with carts and carriages.

Felicity was glad to see that her father's store was bustling. She stood aside as two ladies stepped out of the store's door.

"Terrible!" one lady said to the other. "Tea taxed at three pence a pound! Why, that raises the price high as a cat's back!"

"Indeed!" said the other lady. "The king's tax is unfair!"

Ben was the next person to come out of the store's door. He grinned at Felicity. "You look uncomfortable. Let's be on our way, so you can get your lessons over with," he said.

Felicity sighed. "I'd much rather stay at the store."

Ben stopped grinning. "The store is not so cheerful these days," he said.

"I just heard some ladies grumbling about the tax on tea," said Felicity.

"Aye," said Ben. "More and more people are complaining about the tax. They think the king is wrong to tax us colonists without our agreement."

"What do you think?" asked Felicity.

"I think the king's tax should be stopped," said Ben. "You'd better stop, too, or you'll get mud all over your petticoat." Ben pointed to a puddle in front of Felicity.

"Oh!" exclaimed Felicity impatiently, forgetting all about tea and taxes. She stepped around the puddle awkwardly. "I'm so dressed up I can hardly move. I wish being proper were not so

uncomfortable! I wish I could have a lesson in whistling right now, instead of a lesson in behaving like a lady."

"You'll whistle fine when that loose tooth falls out," said Ben. "How's it coming along? Shall I pull it for you?"

"No, thank you," said Felicity. "I'll wait for it to come out by itself."

"Just as well," said Ben. "Because here we are at Miss Manderly's door."

"Good-bye," said Felicity nervously. She touched her coral necklace for good luck, then knocked.

A smiling lady wearing a lacy, white cap opened the door and greeted Felicity. "Miss Merriman?" she said. "How lovely to meet you. I am Miss Manderly."

There was something about Miss Manderly's eyes and the kindly way she tilted her head, that made Felicity feel a little less nervous. "Good day, madam," she said. "Thank you very much indeed for having me." *There*, she thought with relief, *I've done that much properly.*

"You are most welcome," said Miss Manderly. "Do come in and meet the other young ladies." She led Felicity into a sunny little parlor. Two girls rose from their chairs to greet her. One was very tall and dark-haired. The other was very small and dark-haired. Miss Manderly nodded to the tall girl. "Miss Felicity Merriman, may I present Miss Annabelle Cole," she said. Then she nodded to the smaller girl. "And this is Miss Elizabeth Cole."

"Oh, don't bother to call her Elizabeth," said the tall girl in a bossy way. "She's such a little bit of a thing, we call her 'Bitsy' at home."

Felicity thought "Bitsy" was a perfectly dreadful name. She could tell that Elizabeth hated it, too, though she said nothing. Felicity greeted the two girls. "Good day, Annabelle. Good day, *Elizabeth*," she said. She looked at Elizabeth and grinned. Elizabeth looked surprised.

Annabelle raised one eyebrow. "Your last name is Merriman," she said. "You must be the shopkeeper's daughter." She sniffed, as if there were something wrong with being a shopkeeper's daughter.

Felicity was about to explain that her father's

22

store was not a little shop, but one of the largest and finest stores in all of Williamsburg. But Annabelle turned her back. She flounced over to the writing desk and picked up her quill pen. "Of course, at home in England we had our own governess. I expect we shall have one here, too, if Mama can find a suitable person among the colonists," she said. Then she sighed, "I never thought we'd be taking lessons with a shopkeeper's daughter."

Felicity started to say that she was proud of being a colonist and very proud of her father's store, but Miss Manderly spoke first.

"Young ladies," said Miss Manderly. "Please be seated at the tea table." She sat herself gracefully and continued. "Your parents have trusted me with the important task of preparing you to take your place in society. Our lessons together will be pleasant. But do not forget that they are lessons. You are here to learn."

Felicity glanced over at Elizabeth. Her big, brown eyes were open wide as she listened to everything Miss Manderly was saying.

Miss Manderly went on. "Because it is our first day together, we shall begin with polite conversation. A lady makes her guests feel comfortable. She chats pleasantly about topics that include everyone. It is usually best to begin by asking a question of general interest."

Annabelle spoke up right away. "*I* have a question of general interest," she said. "Will the three of us always have our lessons *together?*"

"Not all the time," answered Miss Manderly.

"Good," said Annabelle. "Because Bitsy and this Miss Merriman are far behind me. My governess taught me fine handwriting. I finished my sampler of stitches long ago. And I had dancing lessons with the finest dance master in England."

Miss Manderly smiled. "All of those skills improve with practice," she said firmly. "And you are also here to practice your best manners. I'm sure that your governess in England taught you the rules of polite behavior. So you know that if you are rude, and break those rules, you will be left out of the best society."

All three girls sat up a little straighter. Miss Manderly paused as a maidservant placed a tea tray on the table without rattling a cup. "Your manners will be observed most closely at tea," said Miss Manderly. "Tea is a ceremony. A gentlewoman must behave perfectly at the tea table, both as a hostess and as a guest. Now I will show you the proper way to serve tea."

"Good heavens!" said Annabelle. "Bitsy and I know how to serve tea! We've watched our mother serve tea hundreds of times!"

"Splendid!" said Miss Manderly calmly. "Then you will be quite at ease, won't you?"

Annabelle was quiet.

Miss Manderly opened the tea caddy made of dark, polished wood. Felicity smelled the spicy, smoky scent of tea. Miss Manderly neatly filled the silver caddy spoon five times and put the loose tea leaves into the delicate china teapot. Carefully, she poured hot water from the kettle onto the tea leaves. She put the pretty blue and gold lid on the teapot with a sure and graceful hand. Miss Manderly made it look so lovely that Felicity itched to try preparing the tea herself.

"Hand each guest her cup,

saucer, and spoon," Miss Manderly said, as she did so. "And when the tea is ready, pour it very carefully." Felicity held her teacup and saucer steady as Miss Manderly filled it. "Offer your guest milk or sugar to put in her tea," said Miss Manderly. "Then offer her a cake or a biscuit."

"Oh, these are queen cakes!" said Annabelle as  she took a small cake filled with currants from the plate. "I have heard they are a favorite of the queen in England."

Miss Manderly held the plate of biscuits and queen cakes out to Felicity. Felicity took the smallest biscuit she saw. Miss Manderly smiled. "A wise choice. Hard biscuits don't shed crumbs the way cakes do," she said. "And remember, you are not drinking tea because you are thirsty or eating because you are hungry. The tea is offered to you as a sign of your hostess's hospitality. If you refuse tea, you are refusing her generosity."

"Oh, I would never refuse!" Felicity said. "You make the tea ceremony look so very *pretty*."

"Thank you, my dear," smiled Miss Manderly. "But you may not wish to drink tea all afternoon!

There is of course a polite way to show that you have had *enough* tea. Merely turn your cup upside down on your saucer and place your spoon across it. That is a signal to your hostess that you do not wish to take more tea. And the correct phrase to say is, 'Thank you. I shall take no tea.'"

Felicity took a small bite of the hard biscuit. As soon as she chewed, she knew it was a mistake. Her loose tooth fell out and landed—Plop! Clink!— in her cup of tea. Felicity stared down at it. She didn't know what to do or say. No one else did either, not even Miss Manderly. The silence was very long. *Oh, dear,* thought Felicity. *I'm sure dropping your tooth in your tea breaks all the rules of polite behavior!*

Felicity felt terrible. But then Elizabeth started to giggle quietly, in a way that made Felicity smile, then giggle with her. Miss Manderly was laughing, too. Her eyes were sparkly. "Well!" she said. "I am afraid I do *not* know the polite thing to say when your tooth falls into your tea!" She turned to the maidservant. "Please take away Miss Merriman's teacup," she said. "But do return the tooth." Miss Manderly smiled, and Felicity felt fine.

*Felicity's loose tooth fell out and landed—
Plop! Clink!—in her cup of tea.*

When the tea tray was cleared away, Annabelle went off to practice writing fancy capital letters. Miss Manderly wrote out a phrase for Elizabeth and Felicity to copy into their copybooks:

Think ere you speak
for Words, once flown,
Once utter'd, are
no more your own.

Miss Manderly sat back and read it aloud, "'Think ere you speak, for words, once flown, once uttered, are no more your own.' I would like you to practice writing this phrase," she said. "The word 'ere' means 'before.' The phrase tells you to think before you speak. And I think it is a good idea to think before you write, too." She smiled, then left to help Annabelle.

Felicity grinned at Elizabeth. "My mother is forever telling me to think before I speak and think before I act. She says I just gallop into everything with no more thought than a wild pony." Felicity dipped her quill pen in the inkwell she shared with Elizabeth. But instead of writing, she sketched a horse in her copybook. She picked up the sander and sprinkled pounce on the ink to dry it.

Elizabeth looked at Felicity's sketch. "Oh, I love horses," she said. She asked shyly, "Do you?"

"More than anything," said Felicity. "Once I had a horse. I mean, once I had a horse for a while." She told Elizabeth about Penny, the horse she had tamed. "I wanted to keep her, but she didn't belong to me. Her owner beat her, and she ran away. The truth is, I helped her run away. But I still think about her all the time."

Elizabeth's eyes were round and shiny. "That's the saddest, bravest thing I ever heard," she said. "Will Penny ever come back?"

"Maybe," said Felicity. "I hope so."

"I think she will," said Elizabeth firmly. "I'm sure she will, someday."

Felicity smiled at her. Elizabeth was going to be a good friend, a very good friend.

The girls were having such a good time writing and talking about horses, they were surprised when Miss Manderly said it was time to go home.

"Young ladies," said Miss Manderly. "At home this evening I would like you to practice writing invitations. Please pretend that you are inviting each other to tea. Write proper invitations in your copybooks. Use your best penmanship. At our next lesson, I will check your work. You may go now."

"Come along, Bitsy," said Annabelle in her bossy way.

Elizabeth started to say something to Annabelle, then waved and called, "Good day, Felicity!" instead.

"Good day, Elizabeth!" Felicity answered. She hurried home full of excitement. She could not wait to tell Mother and Nan about her afternoon.

Nan hopped up to greet Felicity when she came home. "What are the lessons like? And what is Miss Manderly like?" she asked eagerly.

"Miss Manderly is lovely," said Felicity. She sank into her chair with a happy sigh. "I hope I can learn to be like her."

"And the two girls from England?" asked Nan.

"The younger one, Elizabeth, is very fine," said Felicity. "She is just my age. But I don't like her older sister, Annabelle. She is a snob. She acts as if I am not as good as she is because my father owns a store. I'm supposed to write Annabelle an invitation to tea, to practice my writing. I'm not going to do it."

"You *must* do it," said Mrs. Merriman.

"Oh, but a proper invitation would say that I request the favor of her company," said Felicity. "And I don't *like* Annabelle's company."

Mrs. Merriman handed Felicity her copybook and the inkstand with the quill pen, inkwell, and sander. "We must often be with people we might not choose as company," said Mrs. Merriman. "A gentlewoman is kind to everyone."

"But Annabelle is rude," said Felicity. "She treated me badly because I am a colonist. She thinks colonists are uncivilized!"

"Then you must be perfectly polite," said Mrs. Merriman. "You must show her that we colonists are indeed civilized."

"Very well," grinned Felicity. She picked up the quill pen and dipped it in the ink. "I'll do it to show Annabelle how wrong she is."

TEA IN THE RIVER

"Why, Felicity!" exclaimed Miss Manderly
at their next lesson. "Your invitations look
lovely! What fine handwriting!" She
handed back Felicity's copybook with a smile.
Elizabeth smiled at Felicity, too.

Felicity beamed. She was proud of the
invitations. She had practiced over and over again,
until she was sure she could write the words
perfectly. She forced herself to be slow and careful
when she wrote in her copybook. Felicity was
determined to show snobby Annabelle that she was
just as accomplished and well-mannered as any
gentlewoman in England.

As the weeks went by, Felicity grew to enjoy

her lessons with Miss Manderly more and more. She especially loved teatime. It was a peaceful part of the day when nothing rude or unsettling could happen. The tea tray was beautiful, with blue china cups as delicate as flowers and shiny spoons in their lovely china spoon boat. Felicity memorized Miss Manderly's graceful movements as she measured the tea out of the caddy. She longed to use the caddy spoon and to pour the steaming water into the pretty teapot. Sometimes Miss Manderly asked her to hand around the cups and offer the milk and sugar. Felicity was very careful. She couldn't wait until it was her turn to prepare and pour the tea herself. She wanted to do it perfectly.

Felicity still loved to run and play out of doors. She was still quite often too lively to be ladylike. But at lessons, Felicity tried to keep her voice low and her back straight and her teacup balanced. She remembered to laugh softly and ask polite questions. She began to enjoy being on her best behavior at tea. Elizabeth and Felicity always had a great deal to say to each other. But Miss Manderly insisted they discuss questions of general interest.

That meant they had to include Annabelle in their conversations. Annabelle was not very interesting. But she usually tried to be pleasant at teatime. She was almost always polite in front of Miss Manderly.

But one day at teatime, Miss Manderly left the room for a moment. Annabelle heaved a big sigh. "Well," she said. "Soon we won't have any tea to drink if these uncivilized colonists have their way."

"What do you mean?" Felicity asked.

"Haven't you heard?" asked Annabelle in a mean voice. "A few days ago in Yorktown, a mob of colonists threw chests of tea into the river. The tea was on a ship that had come from England."

"But why did they do it?" asked Felicity.

"Because they are hot-heads!" said Annabelle. "They were a wild mob!"

"They didn't hurt anybody," Elizabeth said to Felicity softly.

"Quiet, Bitsy!" snapped Annabelle. Elizabeth shrank back. Annabelle went on. "The colonists destroyed the tea because they did not want to pay the king's tax on it. I've always said these colonists

are ungrateful for all our king has done for them.
I've always said—"

Just then, Miss Manderly returned. Annabelle
stopped talking. She smiled sweetly at Miss
Manderly.

Felicity did not know what to think. Could
Annabelle be right? It was surely wrong for
colonists to destroy tea they did not own. But
wasn't the king's tax wrong, too? She looked down
into her tea and said nothing.

Felicity was still quiet as she and Elizabeth
walked home after lessons. They always hurried

ahead of Annabelle so that they could talk.

"Lissie," said Elizabeth kindly. "It wasn't you or your family who threw the tea into the river. You shouldn't feel bad about what those other colonists did. It's not your fault."

"I know," said Felicity. "But Annabelle makes me so angry. She thinks colonists are no good."

Elizabeth smiled a little. "I know one colonist Annabelle admires," she said quietly. "Ben, your father's apprentice."

Felicity stopped. "Ben?" she asked. "Annabelle likes Ben?"

"Aye," nodded Elizabeth. "Annabelle thinks he is handsome. And she found out that he is from a wealthy family. So she admires him."

Felicity laughed. "So that's why she lurks around the store and flutters her eyelashes at Ben like a ninny. Oh, wait till I tell Ben that Annabelle is sweet on him!"

"Oh, you mustn't tell Ben!" said Elizabeth. "Annabelle would be so angry if you did!"

"I won't tell him," said Felicity. "Don't worry."

Felicity and Elizabeth waited at Mr. Merriman's store for Annabelle to catch up. They chatted about their lessons, and horses, and their samplers. But whenever they thought about Annabelle being sweet on Ben, they began to giggle. It was very hard not to laugh when Annabelle came into the store. She looked around. When she saw Ben was not there, she said briskly, "Come along, Bitsy! There's no need to stay!"

Felicity and Elizabeth smiled at each other and waved good-bye.

Soon after Elizabeth and Annabelle had left, Mr. Merriman began to close up the store. "You and Elizabeth are the merriest girls in Virginia," he said. "You always have a great deal to talk about."

"Aye," said Felicity. "Today we had a  wonderful idea for something to put on our samplers. Miss Manderly says we're to start them soon. We are going to need lots of red silk thread."

"Are you going to stitch some red Virginia roses, red as the roses in my lovely Lissie's cheeks?" asked Mr. Merriman.

"Oh, no," said Felicity. "Elizabeth says we should put a bright red crown right at the top of our samplers to show that we all look up to the same king. She says that he is fair and generous to everyone he rules, in England and in his colonies."

"Well," said Mr. Merriman with a sad smile. "I am not sure everyone would agree. Many people feel the king is treating us colonists badly. They do not want to be ruled by the king anymore."

Felicity was confused. "But isn't that *disloyal?*" she asked.

Mr. Merriman shrugged. "People will not be loyal to someone who treats them unfairly. And they feel the king's tax on tea is unfair."

"Annabelle said some colonists threw tea into the York River," said Felicity. "Is that true?"

"Yes," said Mr. Merriman. "It was their way of showing the king they are angry. Other people have decided they are not going to buy tea or even drink it anymore. That will be *their* way to show the king that they are angry."

"Just because they have to pay a few pence more for tea?" asked Felicity.

"It isn't only the tax on tea," answered Mr. Merriman. "We colonists built this country with our own hard work. Many people feel we should govern it ourselves, without the king."

Without the king? Felicity couldn't imagine it. "Do you think we would be better off without the king, Father?" she asked.

Mr. Merriman sighed. "That is the question everyone is asking."

Felicity looked up at him. "Miss Manderly would call it a question of general interest," she said.

"Quite so," said Mr. Merriman. "And I do not know the answer to it."

"Well, do you think I should not stitch a crown on my sampler?" Felicity asked her father.

Mr. Merriman handed her some red silk thread. "I think you must answer that question for yourself," he said. "Now come along, my child. 'Tis time we were on our way home."

BANANABELLE

Felicity did not say anything to Elizabeth about the talk she'd had with her father about the king and tea. She was too confused and uncomfortable. She did not decide what to do about her sampler, either. She made a few stitches with the red thread at the top of her sampler, but they didn't look like a crown, that was for certain. They looked like bumpy knots.

"Oh, no!" she exclaimed. "I've tangled my thread *again!* I shall have to cut it and start all over." She and Elizabeth were working on their samplers at Elizabeth's house one cold, November afternoon.

"My mother has some scissors in her chamber,"

said Elizabeth. "Let's go and fetch them."

"Will we disturb your mother?" asked Felicity.

"Oh, no," said Elizabeth. "She and Annabelle have gone out calling. They won't be home for hours. Follow me."

Felicity and Elizabeth went up the wide staircase to Mrs. Cole's bedchamber. "She keeps the scissors in her sewing basket," said Elizabeth. "Over here, next to her wigs."

"I've never seen so many wigs and curls outside the wigmaker's shop," said Felicity. She looked at the five carved, wooden heads lined up in a row. "Do you think I might try a wig on?" she asked boldly.

"Well, I suppose so," said Elizabeth.

Felicity took a wig of dark hair off one of the heads. "I have always wanted to see what I would look like with dark hair," she said. She gazed at herself in the looking glass and giggled. "I look like a ninny!"

Elizabeth giggled. "Oh, Lissie, you *do* look funny!"

Felicity loved to make Elizabeth laugh. She picked up the bald, wooden head and fluttered her eyelashes at it, just like Annabelle. "Oh, my darling Ben!" she said in a high voice. "It is I, your beautiful Bananabelle! You have stolen my heart away!"

"Bananabelle!" Elizabeth laughed. "You sound just like her!"

Felicity pressed her cheek against the wooden head's cheek. "Let us be married, my darling Ben. And we can discuss questions of general interest all the day long! Oh, I love you, you handsome lad! Say that you love me, your Bananabelle, or I shall die!" She gave the wooden head a big, smacking kiss.

"WHAT'S *THIS?*" Annabelle's voice boomed from the doorway.

Felicity pulled off the wig and whirled around. Elizabeth went white.

Annabelle crossed her arms. "Very amusing," she said in a mean voice. "So this is what you and your rude little shopkeeper friend do, Bitsy."

Elizabeth did not say anything. She looked down at her shoes.

Felicity spoke up. "Oh, Annabelle! It was only a bit of fun," she said.

43

"Oh, my darling Ben!" Felicity said in a high voice.
"It is I, your beautiful Bananabelle!"

"Fun?" snorted Annabelle. "You have no manners! I shall tell Mama what you've done. We shall see if she thinks it is fun. I wouldn't be surprised if she tells Bitsy never to speak to you again!"

Felicity was not afraid of Annabelle. "If you tell your mother," she said coolly, "I will tell Ben you are sweet on him."

"Oh!" sputtered Annabelle. "Oh!" She glared at Felicity. "You . . . you uncivilized brat!" She stormed from the room.

Elizabeth looked at Felicity. Her brown eyes were troubled. "Why did you say that to her?" she asked. "Now she will be angry."

Felicity shrugged. "She is nothing but a bully. I don't care if she is angry. She doesn't scare me. She shouldn't scare you."

"But I'm not like you, Felicity," said Elizabeth. "I'm not brave. Annabelle can be mean sometimes. I've always been afraid of her."

"You don't have to be afraid of her anymore," said Felicity. "I am your friend now. I'll help you. I am not afraid of old Bananabelle."

At last, Elizabeth smiled. "Lissie," she said.

"I'm so glad we're friends."

"Me, too," said Felicity. "But I'd best go along now. Will you walk with me?"

The girls pulled their cloaks close around them, for the wind was sharp. They hurried along to Mr. Merriman's store and ran inside, all out of breath. "Stay for a moment to get warm," Felicity said to Elizabeth.

There were six well-dressed men talking to Mr. Merriman and Ben. One of the men was holding a paper that had a long list of names on it. No one noticed the girls as they slipped into a corner by the fireplace and warmed their hands. Felicity looked up in surprise when she heard her father speaking. He sounded very stern, though his voice was steady.

"Yes, I signed the agreement," said Mr. Merriman. "More than four hundred other merchants around the colonies signed it, too. We have decided not to sell tea anymore. It is our way of showing the king we think the tax on tea is wrong."

"That is disloyal!" shouted the man. "It is wrong for colonists to go against the king! You know it is wrong, Merriman."

Elizabeth and Felicity hid behind a barrel. They were very quiet.

"Gentlemen," said Mr. Merriman firmly. "Do not tell me what to do in my store. I will do what my heart and my reason tell me is right."

"And what of those hot-heads in Yorktown? Do you think they were right to toss good tea into the river?" said another man.

"They threw that tea away to send a message to the king," said Mr. Merriman. "They did what they thought was right."

"They were *wrong* to toss that tea!" said the man angrily. "And you are wrong to stop selling tea."

"Aye!" said another man. "You are making a grave mistake. You'll get no more of my money, Merriman. None of us will ever shop here again! We won't give our business to anyone who isn't loyal to the king. Will we, gentlemen?"

"No!" called out several of the men. The store shook with their shouts.

Felicity turned to look at Elizabeth. But Elizabeth was gone.

"They were wrong to toss that tea!" said the man angrily. "And you, Merriman, are wrong to stop selling tea."

Mr. Merriman's voice was sad. "You gentlemen are my neighbors and my friends," he said as the men left. "I had hoped we could disagree politely, without fighting. Fighting does no good."

Felicity stayed in the corner until all the men were gone and the store was quiet. Her father and Ben were standing silently. Felicity ran up to her father and hugged him. "Father!" she said.

Mr. Merriman held her close. "Did you hear that, my child?" he asked.

"Aye," said Felicity. "Elizabeth and I both did."

"And did it frighten you?" asked Mr. Merriman.

"A little," said Felicity. "Who were those men, Father?"

"Just some men of the town," said her father. "I know most of them."

Ben spoke up. "They are Loyalists," he said. "They are angry because some of us have joined together to protest against the king."

"I've decided to stop selling tea in my store, to show the king we colonists will not pay his tax," explained Mr. Merriman.

"If no one pays the tax, it will make the king

angry," said Felicity. "Won't that start a fight?"

"Aye," said Mr. Merriman softly. "It could."

"Do you think there will be a war?" asked Felicity.

"I don't know," said Mr. Merriman, shaking his head.

"It may take a war to show the king he cannot treat the colonists this way anymore!" exclaimed Ben.

"Hush, boy!" said Mr. Merriman. "You have not seen war, as I have. War is the worst way to solve disagreements. War is like a terrible illness. Everyone suffers. People die. Those who survive are weakened, and 'tis a long while before they are full strength again."

Ben was quiet. Felicity was quiet, too. Then she asked, "Father, will we drink tea at home?"

"No," said Mr. Merriman. "There will be no tea in our house."

"But what should I do at lessons?" asked Felicity. "We drink tea there. And teatime is so very *important*. What will Miss Manderly think if I refuse tea?" She turned to her father with a sad, confused face.

A BRIGHT RED CARDINAL BIRD

Felicity and Elizabeth did not have a chance to talk at lessons the next day. Miss Manderly was working with them on their samplers.

"And what is this at the top of your sampler, Felicity?" Miss Manderly asked. "Such bright red thread. Perhaps you are stitching our Virginia songbird, the cardinal. Is that what you are planning?"

"I . . . I don't know," said Felicity. "I haven't decided."

"Well," said Miss Manderly. "You will have to decide soon, my dear. You cannot leave red knots at the top of your sampler!"

Felicity saw Elizabeth looking at her. The red crown on Elizabeth's sampler was almost finished.

When it was time for tea, Miss Manderly smiled. "Young ladies," she said, "you have made such fine progress. I think the time has come for you to take turns serving the tea. Annabelle, you are the eldest. You shall serve the tea today."

Felicity was nervous. She had not decided what she was going to do about tea, either. Her family wasn't drinking tea at home. Should she drink it here? She watched as Annabelle sat behind the tea table acting very important. After Annabelle prepared the tea, she filled Miss Manderly's cup first, then Elizabeth's cup, and then her own.

Miss Manderly leaned forward in her chair. "Annabelle, my dear," she said. "You have forgotten to serve Miss Merriman her tea."

"Oh!" said Annabelle, holding her cup daintily. "I was only thinking of the carpet."

"The carpet?" asked Miss Manderly.

"Yes, indeed," said Annabelle. She put her nose in the air. "I did not serve Felicity because I did not want her to toss the tea out all over your fine carpet."

Felicity felt her face getting red.

"Annabelle!" gasped Miss Manderly. "Apologize at once!"

"Oh, but Felicity would be proud to toss out her tea," said Annabelle. "Her father said it was *right* to toss out tea. He said those hot-heads in Yorktown were right to throw the tea into the river."

"No!" cried Felicity. "My father didn't say that! He—"

"Yes, he did!" snapped Annabelle. "Bitsy heard him. Didn't you, Bitsy?"

Elizabeth didn't say anything.

"But that's *not* what he said," cried Felicity. "Tell her, Elizabeth!"

Elizabeth would not look at Felicity.

Felicity tried to explain. "My father said the men who threw the tea into the river thought that they were right. They did it to show the king that they did not agree with the tax on tea."

"Your father disagrees with the king's tax, too!" said Annabelle. "That's why he's not going to sell tea in his store anymore. He is disloyal to the king. Your father is a *traitor!*"

"No!" shouted Felicity. "My father is not a traitor!" She jumped up from her chair and knocked against the tea tray. The teapot teetered and the cups and saucers rattled. Felicity grabbed her sampler frame in her fist and ran out of the room. She slammed the door behind her.

Felicity was in a red rage. Home she stormed, away from Miss Manderly's prim little house, through the crowded, dusty streets. *How could Elizabeth do it? How could she?* she kept asking herself. It was Elizabeth she was most angry at. *Why didn't she tell Annabelle the truth? Father was only trying to be fair. Father is not the one who is a traitor,* thought Felicity. *Elizabeth is the traitor— to me!*

Felicity burst into the house and pounded up the stairs to her room. She curled up on her bed in a tight roll. Her sampler was loosened and wrinkled. She could not think. She was too mad to cry. Anger boiled inside her. Elizabeth was supposed to be her friend. Instead, she let Annabelle tell hateful lies about her father. *I hate Annabelle,* she thought, *and I hate Elizabeth, too. I don't want to see either of them ever again.*

"No!" shouted Felicity. "My father is not a traitor!"

Felicity heard the door open. "Lissie?" whispered her mother. She sat on the bed and put Felicity's head in her lap. "What is it, my child?"

her mother asked softly. She smoothed Felicity's hair. "What is it, Lissie, my dear?"

Felicity took a shaky breath. "Elizabeth and Annabelle think Father is a traitor. I don't want to speak to them ever again," she said.

"Ahhhh," said her mother sadly. "It's because of the argument about tea, isn't it?"

Felicity nodded.

Mrs. Merriman sighed. "My poor child," she said. "I fear there is more of this trouble coming. This talk against the king will cause nothing but sorrow before it is over. It will divide families and destroy friendships, if we let it." Gently, she took Felicity's sampler from her hands.

"Throw that away!" said Felicity. "I hate it. It is full of mistakes."

Mrs. Merriman pulled the sampler taut in its frame. "No, my impatient one," she said calmly. "I see a great deal that's good in this sampler. It would be a terrible waste to throw it all away because of one mistake or two." She looked at Felicity. "I think it would be a terrible waste to throw away your friendship with Elizabeth, too, because of one misunderstanding."

"How can I be Elizabeth's friend?" asked Felicity. "She thinks Father is a traitor to the king!"

"Did she say that?" asked her mother.

"No, Annabelle did. But Elizabeth did not stop her," said Felicity.

"Elizabeth is not as brave as you are," said Mother. "You must be patient with your friend, Lissie."

"She's not my friend!" said Felicity. "If she were my friend, she wouldn't have let Annabelle say such awful things!"

"I see," said Mother. "You are afraid Elizabeth does not like you anymore. Is that it?"

"Aye," whispered Felicity.

"I think you are wrong about that," said Mrs. Merriman. "But you will have to go back to your lessons to find out."

"I don't want to go to the lessons anymore!" exclaimed Felicity.

"They are a privilege," said Mrs. Merriman. "It is not wise to walk away from such a chance to learn."

"I want to forget everything I've learned," said Felicity.

"Aye," said Mrs. Merriman, looking down at the sampler. "It is easiest to throw everything away. It is harder to untangle knots and try again." She looked at Felicity with love. "It takes courage."

Felicity thought for a moment. Then she said, "What if I *do* go back? What shall I do when they serve tea? I want to be loyal to Father. I don't want to drink tea anymore. But if I am rude, Miss Manderly won't want me to come back ever again. Elizabeth won't want to be my friend. And Annabelle will think she is right, that colonists *are* uncivilized." Felicity looked at her mother. "What shall I do?"

"Now that is a difficult knot to untangle," said Mrs. Merriman. "You must be well-mannered but follow your heart. You must be polite but do what you think is right." She lowered Felicity's head onto the pillow gently. "Rest now and think about it. I trust you will find a way. You have become quite a gracious young lady these past few weeks." She kissed Felicity's forehead and left quietly.

🦌

It took all the bravery Felicity could muster to walk back into Miss Manderly's house the next day.

Miss Manderly greeted her with a smile. "Good day, Miss Merriman," she said. "I am exceedingly glad to see you today."

"Thank you, Miss Manderly," Felicity said. She sat down and went to work on her sampler. She did not speak to Elizabeth or Annabelle. They did not speak to her.

"Why, Felicity, how lovely," said Miss Manderly. "I see that you have indeed stitched a red cardinal bird at the top of your sampler. It looks just like our proud Virginia cardinals!"

"Oh!" said Elizabeth. "It *is* pretty, Lissie." She looked at Felicity shyly. "Would you mind, I mean, do you think it would be all right if I stitched one just like it on my sampler?" she asked.

"Bitsy!" scolded Annabelle.

Elizabeth whirled around and faced Annabelle.

"I *hate* being called Bitsy," she said firmly. "From now on, call me *Elizabeth.*"

"Why, I—" sputtered Annabelle.

"Or I will call you Bananabelle in front of everyone," said Elizabeth. "Annabelle, Bananabelle."

For once, Annabelle was speechless. Elizabeth grinned at Felicity. Felicity felt her spirits rise like a bird. *Elizabeth is still my friend,* she thought. She smiled at Elizabeth.

Miss Manderly smiled, too. "Well, *Elizabeth,*" she said. "Will you do us the honor of serving tea this afternoon?"

"Yes, indeed!" said Elizabeth.

Felicity's heart pounded as she took her place at the tea table. This was the moment she dreaded. How could she refuse tea without being rude? She watched Elizabeth measure the tea and pour the hot water into the teapot. She watched as Elizabeth handed each of them a teacup, saucer, and spoon. Then Elizabeth began to fill the teacups. She poured Miss Manderly's cup without spilling a drop. She poured Annabelle's cup and offered her the sugar. Felicity's cup was next.

Felicity took a deep breath. Very gracefully, she turned her teacup upside down on the saucer and put her spoon across it. "Thank you, Elizabeth," she said politely in a clear, strong voice. "I shall take no tea."

"Well done," said Miss Manderly softly.

Elizabeth smiled. "Perhaps you'd like a queen cake," she said as she handed the plate to Felicity.

"I'd prefer a plain biscuit," said Felicity as she smiled back at her friend. "I've no loose teeth to worry about today!"

A PEEK INTO
THE PAST

A mother teaching her children in 1756. The hornbook (left) was named for the thin, see-through layer of cow's horn that protected the lesson sheet.

Back in colonial times when Felicity was growing up, there were few schools. Instead, children learned to read and write at home. Parents taught their children to read using a hornbook, and they often practiced reading from the Bible. They learned to write with a *quill pen* made from a feather, dipped into ink made from colored powder and water. To keep the ink from blotting, they sprinkled it with *pounce*, which was like sand. Paper was expensive, so most children practiced writing their letters from one edge to the other in a *copybook*. Often they made the copybooks by sewing sheets of paper together with needle and thread.

Children from wealthy families were taught by a *tutor*, a young man with some college education who lived in the family's house and taught the children. Sometimes the boys, but not the girls, then went to a grammar school where they learned subjects such as geography, Greek, and Latin. The grammar school in Williamsburg was a part of The College of William and Mary. Boys could start there when they were twelve years old and stay in the same school all the way through college.

The Lyon, the Tyger, & the Traveller.

Children looked at penmanship samples when they practiced writing. This inkstand holds the inkwell and sander full of pounce.

It was very important for young girls to learn fancy sewing. This colorful sampler is from England.

But girls like Felicity were given a very different education. People thought girls didn't need to study ideas in books, since they were expected to marry and to run a home. Some people even thought it was impractical for girls to spend too much

The long handle on this fry pan helped protect kitchen workers from the hot cooking fire.

time reading! Instead, mothers taught their daughters the arts of *housewifery*, which included cooking, sewing, and preserving food. Girls had to learn how to manage a household, to direct the work of slaves and servants, and to serve an elegant meal to many people with entertainment afterwards.

Often girls were sent to teachers like Miss Manderly to learn to dance, play musical instruments, and practice fancy stitchery. They were also taught the proper way to serve tea. At tea lessons, they practiced their manners and learned to carry on polite conversation.

A fancy English tea service.

Many of the colonists had come to America from England where tea was a popular drink and teatime was an important hour of the day. The tea ceremony was a reminder of their English background and traditions.

Some teenage boys and girls became *apprentices* like Ben, learning to become shopkeepers or craftsmen by working for a merchant, milliner, blacksmith, or wigmaker.

A LIST of the Names of those who AUDACIOUSLY continue to counteract the UNITED SENTIMENTS of the BODY of Merchants thro'out NORTH-AMERICA; by importing British Goods contrary to the Agreement.

John Bernard,
(In King-Street, almost opposite Vernon's Head.

James McMasters;
(On Treat's Wharf.

Patrick McMasters;
(Opposite the Sign of the Lamb.

John Mein,
(Opposite the White-Horse, and in King-Street.

Nathaniel Rogers,
(Opposite Mr. Henderson Inches Store lower End of King-Street.

William Jackson,
At the Brazen Head, Cornhill, near the Town-House.

Theophilus Lillie,
(Near Mr. Pemberton's Meeting-House, North-End.

John Taylor,
(Nearly opposite the Heart and Crown in Cornhill.

Ame & Elizabeth Cummings;
(Opposite the Old Brick Meeting House, all of Boston.

Israel Williams, Esq; & Son,
(Traders in the Town of Hatfield.

And, Henry Barnes;
(Trader in the Town of M 1670'.

Newspapers printed names of merchants who continued to sell British goods.

Of course, school has never been the only place that people learn. The busy, bustling village of Williamsburg had a newspaper that reported the important events of the times. People in shops, taverns, and private homes talked about the unfair ways the King of England treated the colonists. The colonists were learning to make difficult choices. Many felt that they had worked hard to build lives in America and did not want to be ruled by a king who was far away in England. They did not think it was fair to have to pay taxes to the king for things, like tea, that they bought in stores in America. People, such as the Merrimans, who agreed that the colonies should be independent from England, were called *Patriots*. People, such as the Coles, who still wanted the colonies to be ruled by the king, were called *Loyalists*.

A tea caddy with tea canisters.

One famous Patriot was Thomas Jefferson, who wrote the Declaration of Independence explaining why the colonists wanted to be free from the king's rule. Other Patriots, like

Angry colonists dumped tea from England into the ocean so no one could sell it or drink it.

George Washington and Patrick Henry, came to the Capitol in Williamsburg to discuss forming a new country called the *United States of America*. Imagine what important lessons a nine-year-old girl like Felicity learned every day in that lively place called Williamsburg— lessons about loyalty and independence, about freedom and self-reliance.

Some people think Thomas Jefferson (above) wrote the first draft of the Declaration of Independence in his Windsor writing chair.